The Wrong Fairy Tale

CINDERELLA
and the Seven Dwarfs

First American Edition 2022
Kane Miller, A Division of EDC Publishing

A Raspberry Book
Art direction and cover design: Sidonie Beresford-Browne
Internal design: Andy Bowden and Ailsa Cullen
Copyright © Raspberry Books Ltd 2022

For information contact:
Kane Miller, A Division of EDC Publishing
5402 S 122nd E Ave
Tulsa, OK 74146
www.kanemiller.com
www.myubam.com

Library of Congress Control Number: 2021943716
Printed in China
ISBN: 978-1-68464-379-0
1 2 3 4 5 6 7 8 9 10

The Wrong Fairy Tale

By Tracey Turner
and Summer Macon

CiNDERELLA
and the Seven Dwarfs

Kane Miller
A DIVISION OF EDC PUBLISHING

Once upon a time in the Land of Fairy Tales, the Seven Dwarfs were on their way home after a hard day's work in the gold mine when . . .

THE SEVEN NUGGETS MINE

Meanwhile, Cinderella was in a very bad mood. Her stepsisters had flounced off to a fancy ball at the palace, leaving her to do all the housework.

And there was a lot of it.

She swept,

dusted,

and tidied away.

Then she made a start on the dishes.

When she heard the knock at the door, Cinderella climbed out from under the pile of dishes to answer it. Soon, everyone had introduced themselves. Cinderella told the Seven Dwarfs all about her mean stepsisters.

"You have to do absolutely everything?" asked Helpful.

"That's not fair!" said Tidy.

"Why couldn't you go to the palace too?" asked Dreamy.

Cinderella sighed. "Oh, you have to wear a ball gown, and I don't have one of those. Plus," she muttered quietly, "technically, I don't have an invitation."

Snappy had an idea.
"Wait. We can make a ball gown!"

Everyone set to work.

Snappy designed
the pattern.

Helpful took
measurements.

Choppy cut it out.

All the dwarfs helped to
sew the dress together.

Then Choppy styled Cinderella's hair.

What about shoes?

Cinderella's own shoes were old and scruffy, and she liked the look of the dwarfs' boots. "What size do you take, Helpful?" she asked. Helpful was, of course, happy to help.

"You **shall** go to the ball!" chorused the Seven Dwarfs. "**Hop aboard!**"

"Hang on," said Cinderella. "Seven Dwarfs work in an underground mine . . ."

The palace ballroom was filled with guests by the time Cinderella arrived.

Dancers waltzed past in fabulous clothes dripping with gold and precious stones. Waiters offered trays of delicious-looking cupcakes and fizzy drinks.

That tiara is SO last season!

Cinderella liked the cupcakes. But she wasn't sure about the dancing. And she didn't like all the whispering. Slowly, she made for the door, hoping the dwarfs hadn't gone home.

She was just

t-i-p-t-o-e-i-n-g…

… through the
Grand Entrance Hall when …

CREAK!

"STOP!"

cried a palace guard.

They must have found out that she wasn't invited! Cinderella **ran**.

Cinderella flew down the palace steps to the driveway but caught her foot in a jewel-encrusted drain cover.

"Sorry, Helpful!" she cried, yanking her foot free of the boot and leaping onto the cart.

"Phew!" said Cinderella as they arrived at her house. "That was FUN. Thank you all for a wonderful evening."

"The palace was amazing!" said Dreamy.

"I'm glad we lost those guards!" said Speedy.

"Helpful, I'm sorry about your boot," said Cinderella. "I'll find a way to get it back."

Everyone waved goodbye and promised to visit very soon.

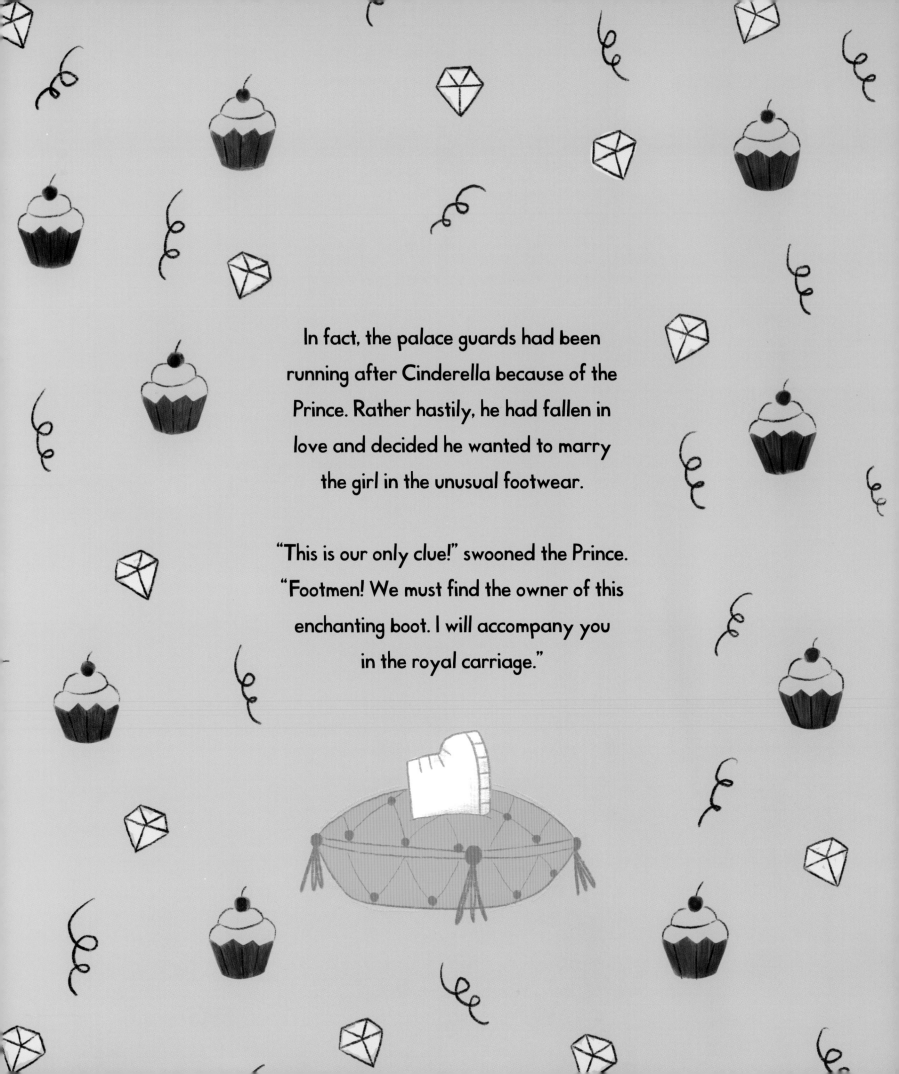

In fact, the palace guards had been running after Cinderella because of the Prince. Rather hastily, he had fallen in love and decided he wanted to marry the girl in the unusual footwear.

"This is our only clue!" swooned the Prince. "Footmen! We must find the owner of this enchanting boot. I will accompany you in the royal carriage."

When the footman knocked on her cottage door,
Cinderella was delighted see the boot.

It's Helpful's
boot!

She gave directions to the
Seven Dwarfs' house.

Luckily, it was the Seven Dwarfs' day off. They were very surprised when they opened the door to a royal footman carrying Helpful's boot on a velvet cushion.

The dwarfs decided to visit Cinderella to tell her the good news about the boot. This time, her stepsisters were at home.

"Who are **you**?" snapped Annabella. "Where's your carriage?"

"You can't let in just any old riffraff!" said Clarabella.

"Honestly," said Cinderella. "Why do I put up with you two?"

Cinderella had realized that the dwarfs were sitting on a gold mine.

All they needed was a good manager.

They made their fortune, built two very
grand houses, and lived happily ever after.
Even though it was completely
the WRONG FAIRY TALE.

THE END